A New Home for Maggie

Written by: Gail Salazar
Illustrated by: Susan Waldrep

My name is Gail Salazar, better known as "Grandma Gail". I became an author after taking in foster children. I am a firm believer in following your dreams and that is exactly what happened to me.

One night I had a dream that I was a writer, and that I wrote books which would help children through their troubled times. So I sat down the very next day and wrote seventeen stories.

I hope that children will relate to these books. They are all about dogs that go through problems in their lives that might be similar to the problems children face; love, loss, friendship, foster care, etc. I hope you will enjoy this story and look forward to the next one.

One day a nurse named Ellie came to our home to care for a friend. As she was leaving I just had to ask her if she had any pets, especially dogs because I write the K-9 Club Stories. Ellie told me about her very special dog Maggie.

Meet Maggie; she is a cute little Schnauzer and this is her story.

3

Maggie was a cute little Schnauzer puppy who lived with her human friend Jane. They were very happy. Jane would take Maggie everywhere she went.

One day while they were out for a walk in the park Jane met someone. His name was Jack. Jack seemed very nice and started spending a lot of time with Jane and Maggie. They would go on bike rides together through the park and down by the river.

Maggie loved the wind blowing
through her hair as she rode in the basket
on Jane's bike. Jane would always pack
a picnic lunch for the three of them. She would
always pack something special for Maggie like
doggie treats shaped into little bones.

Maggie and Jack would go shopping together,
or just sit at home on the couch
watching television. Life seemed really good.

Then one day a big moving van pulled up in front of the house; it was Jack! Jane was very excited. She said that Jack was moving in. Maggie got excited too. She began jumping up and down barking because Jane seemed so happy.

Wow! Jack sure brought a lot of things with him! Jane said she hoped that it would all fit into the house!

Jack sure was a lot of fun. When he was off from work the three of them spent lots of time together. They went to the park to play catch and Jack would always bring her treats. But sometimes Maggie missed the times when she and Jane were together all by themselves without Jack.

Then one day Jack lost his job. This was when things started to change. Jane seemed to be gone at work all the time. Jack started to change too. Instead of playing with Maggie he began to get grouchy and mean. Maggie had always been allowed to sleep in the bedroom with Jane and Jack. But now that Jane was gone all the time Jack just closed the door and kept her out. Maggie started to feel very sad and lonely.

No, Jack wasn't fun anymore. He threw a rug on the floor in the livingroom and told her to sleep there. "And don't you dare get on the couch!" he ordered!

Things kept getting worse. Jack started drinking a lot and yelling more and more. He would leave poor Maggie outside for hours and hours and forget she was even there.

When Jane got home late at night she would find Maggie sitting on the back steps, wet and shivering in the cold. Jack wouldn't even remember to feed Maggie anymore.

Jane was very upset and asked Jack why he wasn't taking care of Maggie. This just made Jack even angrier and he started being mean to Jane too.

"You love that dog more than me!" he would yell. Sometimes he would get so angry he would even hit Jane. This scared Maggie so much that she would run and hide under a chair. But Jane would always come and find her. She would pet Maggie and tell her not to worry, that everything would be okay.

Jane told Maggie that Jack was just feeling bad because he didn't have a job. "Everything will be better when Jack goes back to work," she'd say.

But Jack didn't go back to work and things didn't get better. One day in the middle of winter Jack threw Maggie right outside and it was freezing cold! There was no place for her to go to keep warm. Maggie didn't know what to do; it would be hours before Jane got home from work.

Maggie waited by the door, shivering, for as long as she could. Her feet hurt from standing on the slippery ice and she knew she was going to freeze.

Maggie knew that she only had one chance. She had to go and look for Jane! Maybe she would be on her way home from work by now.

Maggie walked down the street through the snow that was blowing so hard she couldn't see where she was going. Finally, she just couldn't walk any farther. She fell on the ground and just laid there. She was so cold she couldn't get up.

Then Maggie woke up. She was in a strange place that she had never seen before and she felt very frightened. She heard voices coming from the other room, but she didn't know who they were.

Soon a friendly lady walked into the room and talked to Maggie very gently.
"It's okay, little dog," she said, "You're in an animal rescue shelter. We found you lying almost frozen in the snow and brought you here where you can be safe."

Maggie felt very warm and safe for the first time in a long time!

It took a few days for Maggie to get better. She had frost bite on her nose, ears and paws. The people at the shelter looked at Maggie's dog tags to see where she belonged. Maggie wasn't sure she really wanted to go home. She loved Jane and missed her, but she was still afraid of Jack.

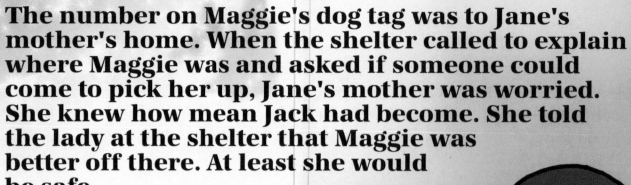

The number on Maggie's dog tag was to Jane's mother's home. When the shelter called to explain where Maggie was and asked if someone could come to pick her up, Jane's mother was worried. She knew how mean Jack had become. She told the lady at the shelter that Maggie was better off there. At least she would be safe.

The people at the shelter felt very sorry for Maggie when Jane's mother told them all the bad things that had happened.

The friendly lady with the gentle voice told Maggie that she was in a safe place and that they were going to find her a new home. They could not understand how anyone could mistreat a nice little dog like Maggie.

Weeks went by and winter was almost over but Maggie still didn't have a new home. Then one day a nurse named Ellie came to the shelter. She wanted to find a friendly little dog that she could take home to her children. When she spotted Maggie she knew right away that this was the dog for her!

19

Maggie was so excited about meeting her new family and a little scared too. But when Ellie took Maggie home the kids fell in love with her right away! Maggie loved them too. She wasn't scared anymore; she had found a new family.

Maggie was happy again.
She loved playing in the park
with the kids, or just piling on the
couch with everyone watching television. But every
once in a while Maggie still missed Jane
and wondered if she was okay.

Ellie and her husband had two children and now they have Maggie whom they love very much. Maggie has been a part of Ellie's family for over ten years now and she loves her adopted family very much.

10369575R00014

Made in the USA
Charleston, SC
29 November 2011